Broken

Stacey Broadbent

Published by Stacey Broadbent, Ashburton, NZ
Copyright 2018 © Stacey Broadbent

*Originally part of the Scars to your Beautiful Anthology under the title "Cut"
*
This is the extended version.

Proofreading by Spell Bound
Cover image from Deposit Photos
Cover Design by Stacey Broadbent
Font: Open Dyslexic

ISBN: 978-0-473-64211-2 (paperback)
          978-0-473-64212-9 (Kindle)
          978-0-473-64442-0 (paperback IS)
          `978-1-0670111-5-4 (Dyslexia Friendly)

Broken

Stacey Broadbent

Contents

Trigger Warnings

This story may contain triggers for some people. It contains scenes of self-harm, violence, and anxiety. Topics of grief are discussed too.

Please seek help from a medical professional if you or someone you know may suffer from depression or anxiety.

NZ:

Helpline: 0800 543 354 or TXT 1737

Website: www.lifeline.org.nz

Author's Note

The characters in this story are from New Zealand, therefore UK spelling and terms have been used. Please remember these are not errors, it's just the way we do things here.

Chapter One

"Just one more time. One more time, and I won't do it again," I reason with myself as I jimmy the blade from my pencil sharpener. Tears blur my vision as I fumble with the tiny screwdriver. I need that release, that feeling of numbness I've come to crave so intensely.

My hands shake as I pull the blade from its holder, brandishing it as if I am Arthur pulling the sword from the stone. I can feel the tension coursing through my veins as I pull up my shirt, tucking it into my bra. Taking a deep breath, I hold the blade to my skin, just to the side of my stomach, closer to my ribcage. I have to find places that are hidden, that no one will see.

They wouldn't understand. I learned that the hard way.

The first time I'd cut on purpose was just superficial slices on my arms, barely breaking the skin. I'd been careless, criss-crossing them all up my forearm—a place that can be seen so easily. Mum freaked out when she caught sight of the red lines adorning my skin, the lines that made me feel, made me focus.

At first, it'd been an accident. I'd been hiding in the library, waiting for the gang of girls who ruled the school to give up and leave me alone. They'd threatened to beat me up, so I went where I knew they'd never go; the library. Miss Hill ruled her library with an iron fist and wouldn't put up with any silly business, so I knew I'd be safe there. I'd sat at a table right in the middle, making sure there were people around me at all times. With nothing better to do, I'd pulled my homework from my bag and started working on my algebra. I could hear their taunts through the window though. They made sure of that. Every few minutes I'd hear them sneering, saying they'd be waiting for me, that I couldn't escape them. It became hard to concentrate on my work. The numbers jumped around on the page until I couldn't make them out anymore. Shuffling pages back and forth, I'd managed to slice myself on the edge of one of my worksheets, and it was as if a valve had been opened inside me. The sting of the cut gave me something to focus on. Their words drowned out by the sound of blood rushing in my ears. I sat there, staring at the tiny slice and the blood that pooled when I squeezed it. Something about it calmed me. Suddenly their words didn't hurt anymore.

I felt numb.

A week later, another slew of abuse thrown my way, and I found myself back in the library. Only this time, I hid in one of the back corners. I was sick of hearing them, couldn't take it any longer, and before I knew it, I held a pair of scissors in my hand. The cool edge of the sharp steel pressed against my skin. The tingle of anxiety ran through my veins and settled in the pit of my belly. Could I really do this? Could I really press the sharp edge to my skin and draw blood?

With one quick motion, I pulled the blade towards me, a thin line of red trailed behind. The relief was instant. The all-encompassing feeling of nothing. No pain, no sorrow, just... nothing.

It lasted for the briefest of moments, but it was enough to make me want more. To *need* more. Rolling my sleeve up, I'd sliced again, and again. One over the other, until I had about a dozen lines all crossing one another. I didn't feel a thing. Just the hollow emptiness that allowed me to breathe again.

I hadn't meant for Mum to see it. I'd come home from school, thrown my bag by the door and marched straight to my room, as I always did. Mum had followed me, reminding me of my chores that I'd neglected to do the night before, giving me yet another reason to feel useless. One more person who thought I was a waste of space. I turned my back on her, slipping my earphones in my ears and pressing play. She grabbed my wrist and turned me to face her. My sleeve slid up my arm and the first of my cuts were poking out for her to see. I'll never forget the look of shock on her face. The way she gasped and twisted my arm closer to her as she yanked my sleeve up farther. The way her eyes filled with tears as she dropped my arm and took a step back, shaking her head. Her lips moved, forming the words, "What have you done?"

I pushed my sleeve back down, gripping the cuff with my fingers and holding it firm in my palm, as if hiding it would make her stop looking at me like that. "I'm sorry," I remember saying, when really, I wasn't sorry for what I'd done.

How could I be sorry for making my pain go away?

"Why?" she asked, her hand coming up to cover her mouth, perhaps to stop her from saying anything else.

I shrugged, not sure what to tell her. "I felt bad."

"So, you cut yourself?" Her brow furrowed in confusion, and she shook her head. "I don't understand. Why would that make you feel better?"

I stared at her, a blank expression on my face, because I knew no matter what I said, it would be wrong.

"What did you use?"

"Scissors." She held her hand out, palm up, waiting for me to hand them over. "They're in my bag." Her eyes flicked around my room, probably searching for anything sharp.

"Do I need to search this room?" Her voice waivered and it made me feel bad that I'd upset her.

"No." I shook my head.

"Good." She sniffed. "We need to dress that, or it will get infected. Did you clean it?" Fix-it-Mum to the rescue. Not so good at giving comfort, but in her element when it comes to keeping things in their place and as they should be. Always the first one there with a first aid kit at the ready. Get your clothes all muddied up on the field? Have no fear; Mum will dress you with her selection of clothes she keeps in the car for such moments. Got a stain you need removed? She'll have a trick to get it out in no time. Efficiency, order, and appearances, the three most important things in her life. More important than the husband she let walk out on us both, and definitely more important than the daughter she can't bear to look in the eye. The daughter who seems to be a constant disappointment.

She rushed off to grab her trusty kit, and I turned the music up and settled back on my bed, closing my eyes. She returned, laden with ointments and bandages, and went about fixing me up while I lay there, letting her. It was easier that way. She'd feel better about herself, and I'd get the peace I thought I wanted. We never spoke of it again.

That was two months ago, and since then, I've cut myself one-hundred and forty-six times. Soon to be one-hundred and forty-seven.

Chapter Two

With my coffee turning cold in my hand, I stare out the window watching Tracey pull her hood over her head and trudge down the drive. I wish I could get through to her. I wish I knew how to reach her. Ever since Malcolm walked out, she's become a shadow of her former self. She won't talk to me anymore, and I don't know what to do to help her. I'm barely able to hold myself together as it is.

I'm not sure what she needs. Do I force her to talk to me? Or do I wait it out and hope she'll come back to me like she would when she was younger? Do I tell her she's scaring me? That I don't understand what's going on inside her head? That I don't know who she is anymore?

I get it. I do. Fourteen-year-old girls don't want their mum to be their best friends. They don't want them hanging around and keeping tabs, but what else am I supposed to do? They never prepare you for this stuff when you're pregnant; for all the hurt and anxiety you go through each and every day just trying to do your best and keep them safe. Because that's our number one job; keep them safe at all costs. Not that she sees it that way.

She was always such a sweet girl growing up. Never a harsh word to be said about anyone. Now I'm lucky if I get more than two words out of her. More often than not it's silence, a glare, and a door closed in my face. But deep down, I know that sweet girl is still inside somewhere, and she still needs me, even if she won't admit it.

I don't know where I went wrong. When Malcolm left, I tried to pretend everything was fine, that I was fine. I tried to show her we could still manage without him, that everything would work out in the end. But it was like a switch flipped the second he walked out that door. The light that used to dance in her eyes disappeared, and I don't know how to get it back.

Now, I spend my nights lying here, wondering what she's thinking while she's holed up in her room with her earbuds in, blocking out the world. Wondering if I could've made it easier for her somehow, prevented this.

They say divorce has a massive impact on children, but I'd hoped that maybe she might be able to see that I did everything I could to make it work with Malcolm. How was I to know he had taken a liking to his secretary at work--cliché, I know. That all those late nights working were actually when he was out with her, playing happy families with another man's kids. All because I wasn't affectionate enough. I'd neglected the basic needs of my husband, the vows that we'd made; to have and to hold. But he'd neglected his vows to; through better and worse.

I know I'm not the same woman he married all those years ago; the happy-go-lucky free spirit he fell for. Life had other plans for me, for us, and I can admit I didn't handle them too well. There was a time when I didn't think I would pull through at all and wanted the earth to swallow me up, but then Tracey came along, and she was like the clean slate I needed. A fresh start.

I thought it would rekindle our relationship. Cement it, make it stronger. And for a time, it did. But old wounds resurfaced, and fear took hold of my heart, and I guess he couldn't take it anymore.

I can come across abrasive sometimes, I know that, but it's not because I don't care. If anything, I care too much. So much that I am in a constant state of worry that I might lose the people I love. It's why I never go anywhere without a first aid kit, why I take every refresher course I can about CPR and first aid, and why I'm so pedantic about cleanliness. I had no idea those very actions were the ones that would send Malcolm running out of our lives and into the arms of another woman.

The sheer sorrow that comes with knowing I wasn't enough to keep him with us bogs me down until I feel as though I can't breathe sometimes. I wanted to protect her from that pain. Wanted to protect her from feeling that she wasn't enough, because she was *always* enough, for both of us. It was *me* who wasn't. It's me who is broken.

But how do I protect her from those feelings when I can barely protect myself? When the man I loved with all my being, the man who was meant to be by my side through all the trials and tribulations, sought the warmth of another woman's bed? When he'd willingly chose to be with another family instead of his own?

I wasn't enough to hold our family together and it kills me.

He walked away.

He packed his bags and he left us.

No, not us.

Me. *I* wasn't enough. Not her. Not my Tracey. She didn't ask for this. She doesn't deserve this pain, but I know she feels it. I know because I've removed blades from her room every day since.

Chapter Three

"Hey, freak!"

"Ugly slag!"

"Fat bitch!"

I don't have to look up to know they're talking to me. This is my life now. It has been since Dad left us for that skank at work and her holier-than-thou daughter, Kat Goodall. The bane of my existence. She thinks because *my* dad chose *her* mum it makes her better than me. I don't understand her logic, but her gaggle of friends clearly do because they all join in on the name-calling. Like it wasn't enough for him to leave, I have to put up with their shit too.

Of all the people in the world, why'd it have to be Kat's mum he shacked up with? Year eleven is hard enough as it is without having to endure Kat and her cronies' snide remarks on a daily basis. I've been called anything from slut to loser and back again. They've even labelled me frigid, which completely contradicts their very words, but there's no cure for idiocy as far as I'm aware.

I try to ignore them, rise above and all that jazz, but sometimes it's just so hard. They're in my face every minute of the school day, following me to the bathroom, waiting outside my classes. They spit on me and stick gum in my hair. Some of them shove me, and Kat's even held a knife to my throat once before—she played it off as a joke, but I know better than that. The teachers turn a blind eye and Mum is oblivious, off in her own world of keeping up appearances. It can be pretty lonely sometimes.

"Get a life!" Maggie, my best friend in the universe, and the only one to know how bad it is with Kat, runs to catch up to me, linking her arm through mine. "You okay?"

I nod, there's not much else I can do. "Yeah. I'm fine." I pat the short bob she fashioned for me, self-conscious.

"It looks great. You really suit it." She gives my arm a squeeze. "Not everyone can pull off an Audrey Hepburn bob, but you do. You're a knock-out."

Fast footsteps approach, and then fingers flick at my hair from behind.

"What's wrong? Cat got your tongue?"

"You get attacked by a lawnmower?"

My shoulders tense as their insults wash over me, proving I was right to be insecure. I know I shouldn't add fuel to the fire, but my hands move of their own volition, yanking my hood over my head.

Maggie glances over her shoulder. "I wish they'd all just fuck off and leave you alone. Who the hell does she think she is? Queen bloody Latifah?" She shakes her head, and we pick up the pace. If I don't acknowledge them, they're less likely to get physical.

"That's right, hide your ugly mug. No one wants to see that fugly face!"

Maggie pulls me down another corridor and straight for the library, my safe haven. I swipe a tear from my eye before anyone sees. Miss Hill greets us with a nod, and we head through to the study tables.

"Have you told your mum yet?" Maggie asks, her voice soft and gentle.

I snort. "No, and I'm not going to. It's not like she can whip out a first aid kit and make them stop."

Determined not to discuss it further, I try to think of something to say, something to take my mind off everything before I can't stop myself.

The blade I pulled from a pencil sharpener is already singing my name from the recesses of my bag, but I shake it off, and say the first thing that comes to mind. "How'd you get on with your history test?"

Maggie rolls her eyes and rubs her forehead. "Don't even ask. I swear to God, the information goes in and straight back out again. I have the memory of a goldfish."

"You know, they actually disproved that theory." I carry on, glad for the change in conversation. Distraction is the key. "They did tests where in order to be fed, the fish had to press a lever, and they did it, continually."

"It amazes me the amount of random facts you know. Where were you when I needed the dates of World War I?"

"1914-1918."

Maggie comes to a stop at one of the tables, throwing her bag on the chair. "Seriously? You don't even take history!"

I shrug. "I don't know. I hear things and it just stays in there." I point to my head. "Probably saw it on one of those docos Dad always used to watch." My smile falters. It just slipped out, and now I'm thinking about him and why he hasn't been to see me once since he left.

Maggie rubs her hand down my arm. "It'll get easier." Her parents divorced when she was eight, and they both seem to be happier for it. I guess after a while it will be the same for us. Though Kat might have a thing or two to say about that. Somehow, I don't see us playing happy families anytime soon.

I don't even get why she hates me so much. If anything, it should be me who hates her, not the other way around. She stole my dad.

Maggie takes my hand. "I know it doesn't seem like it right now, but you'll get through this."

I snort derisively. The only way I'm getting through this is if Kat gets off my back, and it'll be a cold day in Hell when that happens.

Janet

Chapter Four

The door to Tracey's room squeaks as I push it open, a siren alerting to what I'm about to do. I take a moment to gather myself before stepping over the threshold. Some might see it as an invasion of privacy, but I see it as protection. It's the only way I know of to keep her safe, and as long as I feel it's necessary, I will continue to do so. Every. Single. Day.

Dragging her heavy curtains to the side, I blink at the glare of light as it flows into the room. With hands on hips, I glance around, my eagle eyes searching for anything out of place. Her bed is made with the precision of a hospital nurse, corners tucked in neatly and not a wrinkle in sight. Shoes lined up against the wall, clothes folded neatly on the chair in the corner. Even her dressing table has been dusted clean, with only a few items left on top. Looking around, you'd be remiss to believe a teenage girl lived here.

It wasn't always so. I remember battling with her to keep her room clean not so long ago, but slowly, over the last few months, she's been withdrawing inside herself, hiding in her room for hours on end. Typical of a girl her age, I know, but I worry that she's become somewhat obsessive. I know that feeling all too well, that need for control, for everything to be in order. I can't help but think I've created a miniature version of me; someone wary and in constant fear.

Fear. Worry. Two simple words that weigh so heavily on the mind, especially as a mother.

They can drive you to do things you never dreamed you would. For instance, rifling through your daughter's drawers to check for anything she could use to harm herself. Anything remotely sharp or easily fashioned into a weapon.

It's a task I never imagined I'd have to complete day in and day out when I saw those two pink lines staring back at me, promising another chance at happiness.

Tracey is smart too. She doesn't hide things in plain sight or obvious places. And she never uses the same spot twice. I've had to see things through her eyes to match her cunning and thwart her plans. There is no doubt in my mind things would be miles worse if I didn't do this, let's face it, despicable job of going through her things. But I will not apologise for trying to keep my baby safe. I will not.

I've even gone so far as to lift her mattress to check for a diary—the worst form of betrayal in a teenage girl's eyes, but I justify it by my need to keep her alive. I don't know what I'd do if anything were to happen to her. I don't think I could pick the pieces up a second time. No mother should have to do that.

Out of habit, I check the spots she's used before; the small ledge on her windowsill, the ring drawer in her jewellery box, the candle holder on her desk, and even her jacket pockets. As I expected, I come up empty. Part of me, the emotional part, wants to rejoice and believe we've come to the end of it all, but the more rational part of me worries she's changed tactics. I was fooling myself to think she wouldn't notice them missing from her room. But where else would she hide them? Not anywhere I could stumble across them. Not anywhere else in the house. Which means... I'm missing something.

Think, Janet, think.

I spin on my heels, trying to see the room through her eyes. Where would I hide something from someone like me? Crouching down low, I take another look around, hoping a different angle might inspire me.

My eyes land on her shoes all lined up neatly. All except one. One pair; her dirty old sneakers. Of course. The mother with a penchant for cleanliness would never think to go near the shoes caked in mud. Little does she know; this mother would do just about anything to keep her daughter from harm.

I drop to my hands and knees, scooting forward. The left shoe is where it should be, pushed up against the wall, but the right is slightly overlapping the left. This is the one I grab. I give it a shake, tipping it upside down. Nothing. I check the laces to see if it's been secured underneath them. Nope. I almost give up until a glint of metal catches my eye. Wedged into the side of the rubber sole is a broken piece of blade from a craft knife.

Tears spring to my eyes as I pull it free, the shoe falling into my lap. Devastation courses through my veins, destroying the tiny ray of hope I've been clutching at, and I realise something.

She's never going to stop.

Chapter Five

"Earth to Tracey." Maggie's hand waves in front of my face. "Are you even listening?"

I blink, focusing on her eyes that are now hovering in my field of vision. "Sorry, I was a million miles away." The truth is, I was back in Chemistry class, trying to ignore the pain of an incessant test tube being prodded into my shoulder blade. My fingers graze across the tender spot. I wouldn't be surprised if there is already the beginning of a bruise.

"Shit, again?" Maggie purses her lips, tugging at the collar of my top. I brush her away.

"It's nothing. Don't worry."

"Tracey—"

"Don't." I shake my head. "I'm not going to Mr. Anderson about it. It'll only make it worse."

"I know, but—" she takes my hand, "—when do you draw the line? When do you say enough is enough? It's been months, Tracey."

I turn my head to gaze across the street. It's so hard to keep it inside when she's looking at me like that.

"It's harassment, and it needs to stop." She steps around to block my view, forcing me to look at her. "It's more than just verbal now. It has been for a while. You shouldn't have to put up with this. No one should."

My stupid eyes betray me as a tear trickles down my cheek, and I brush it away with an angry fist. "It's fine." My voice warbles more than I'd like.

"It's not fine... You're not fine." She whispers that last part, and somehow that makes it worse. Throughout this whole thing, she's had my back, but seeing the pity in her eyes right now? I'm afraid it will break me if I don't look away. I need her on my side, in my corner. I need her to think I'm okay.

With a sniff, I hitch my bag up further on my shoulder and turn on my heels. "I can handle it."

"But that's my point, Trace, you shouldn't have to."

"Oh, well that solves everything, right? I just stop putting up with it?" I shake my head, knowing I'm being a bitch but unable to stop myself. "Thanks, I'll give that a try."

Maggie runs to catch up to me. "I'm going to pretend that didn't happen because I know you're upset right now." She takes a deep breath, letting it out slowly. "Don't try and push away the only friend you have, because I've got news for you. It won't work. You're stuck with me." Her fist comes up between us, waiting. "Don't leave me hanging."

With a strangled laugh, I bump my fist into hers. "Sorry."

She waves her hand as if swatting a persistent fly. "Already forgotten."

We go our separate ways when we reach the field, as we always do. Maggie heads through town, and I make my way through the alley that leads to my street.

With my hands in my pockets and my earphones in, I watch the ground in front of me, my shoes kicking a rogue stone along the path. I've walked this route a million times before, and very rarely do I encounter another person; just the way I like it. No cars tearing past, no people to dodge around. It's just me and my music.

Which is why, I suppose, I don't hear her sneak up behind me.

"Umph." I jerk forward, losing my balance. It all happens so quickly, I don't have time to pull my hands from my pockets, and land with a heavy thud on the concrete. My head hits the ground and bounces back, and I'm sure I've grazed my chin and nose. Tears sting my eyes, but I blink them away, determined not to let her see me cry. I try to stand, but a foot lands on my back, pressing me into the hard surface. I say nothing, knowing it'll only get worse if I speak.

"Look at you," Kat spits. "Pathetic. No wonder your dad chose me instead." Her cackle echoes off the alley walls. "Such a waste of space."

I close my eyes and try to block her out. Maybe if I wish hard enough, she'll disappear.

"Why do you even bother? No one wants you here, you know that, right?" When I don't answer, she draws her foot back and kicks me in the ribs. "Right?"

I cry out in pain, sure that I heard a crack. With her foot off my back, I pull my knees up, curling into a ball to protect myself from any more blows.

She spits on my face with a nasty grin. "Why don't you do us all a favour, and go kill yourself?" She grabs my bag, and in one final attempt to hurt me, she tips everything out on top of me.

I lie in the foetal position until I'm sure she's gone. Slowly pushing up from the ground, I gather my belongings and stuff them back into my bag with one hand, while the other cradles my chest. It hurts just to breathe.

My phone sits just out of my reach, having slipped from my hand when I fell. The screen is smashed. Mum won't be happy about that. I tuck it into my pocket and attempt to tidy myself up before heading home. There's not much I can do about the grazes on my face. Blood trickles from my nose into my mouth, and my chin feels as though it's on fire.

I'll have to slip past Mum so she doesn't see what a mess I am. It'll only end up in twenty questions followed by a lecture, and right now, all I want to do is curl up under the covers and cry.

I wish Dad was here. I know I should hate him for what he did. He left me with her; the overbearing mother who can't keep out of my business. But even so, I still love him and wish he'd come back. I miss him so much, and I wonder if he misses me too, or if Kat is right.

No one wants me around. Not even my own father.

Chapter Six

My hands shake as I wrap the blade in tissue paper then bury it beneath larger pieces of rubbish in the bin. I'm out of my depth here, and not for the first time, I wish Malcolm was here to talk to. He'd know how to handle this, what to do to bring our little girl back.

In retrospect, if Malcolm were here, none of this would've started in the first place. She was always Daddy's girl, following him around like a lost puppy, lapping up all his attention. I'm ashamed to admit I was, at times, jealous of how much of his time he gave her, when so little was reserved for me. They would have Daddy-daughter date days every month. Whenever she had news to share, she would run to him first. They had a special connection, and I was often on the outer. I didn't know how to be like he was; relaxed and warm. I still don't.

When he left, their dynamic changed. The date days stopped, he didn't visit or call, and she became that lost puppy again, but with no one to latch onto. When he left, he not only took a part of me, but a part of her too, and I wish I could somehow fill that gap inside her, but she won't let me in.

I straighten, bracing my hands on the counter and ducking my head. Tears cloud my vision, and I blink them away. Motherhood is so much harder than I imagined it would be. No one warns you. Not once did I see anything about having to do constant room searches to remove sharp objects. I don't recall anyone saying how my entire life would now be dedicated to worrying. Where were those pamphlets?

A spot of grease on the counter catches my eye. I must've missed it when I cleaned up last night. Running the hot tap, I hold my hand underneath, waiting for the warmth to come through. There is a ring of gunk around the base of the faucet. Another thing I missed.

With a sniff, I push the plug into the sink and fill it with hot soapy water. I might not be able to fix my daughter, but I can at least fix the mess in here.

Bunching my hair into a bun on top of my head, I set to work, scrubbing every inch of the kitchen until it sparkles. I pull everything from the shelves, wipe them down, and reorganise I shine the mixer and coffee machine. I rearrange every cup in the cupboard by size and colour. And as I finish each task, I feel a tiny glimmer of relief well up inside. With everything in its place, order is restored, and the tightness in my chest loosens.

Chapter Seven

Mum is on her hands and knees, busy cleaning out the kitchen cupboards when I get back home. I try to sneak past, but she looks up at me with a fake smile, pretending everything is right with the world. Her smile fades when she sees my face, so I tip my head, letting my hair fall across so she can't see the worst of it, and breeze past.

"Tracey?" She gets to her feet, dusting her hands down her front. "What happened to your face?"

I mumble an incoherent answer, hoping it will buy me some time. I can't stomach talking to her right now. In fact, I try to avoid it most of the time. My secret stash of blades keeps disappearing, so I know she's going into my room and looking through my stuff. I bet she wouldn't like it if I did the same thing to her.

She's not the one cutting though.

I push that little voice back down in the deepest recesses of my brain where it belongs. She's the bad guy here, not me. If Dad was still here, none of this would be happening. We'd still be a happy family, and I wouldn't even be a blip on Kat's radar.

Mum ruined everything.

It's not her fault.

But he left us.

She needs you too.

The inner voices battle it out to see who will end up on top. My brain hurts just listening to them, so I grab my earphones and try to drown them out with music. It's too late though. That little seed has been planted. The urge is back again. The urge to make it all go away. Feeling

49

nothing is better than feeling hurt, angry, and betrayed.

Why don't you do us all a favour, and go kill yourself?

Pressing my palms into my eyes, I try to ignore it. Try to push it down like I did earlier, but it's so loud it's almost deafening. No amount of music will drown out these thoughts.

I need it. The release. The numbness.

Unable to take it anymore, I drop to my knees, fumbling with the shoes lined up against the wall, hoping beyond hope that she hasn't found it. But she has. I throw the offending shoe across the room with a guttural scream. My eyes dart around, knowing there's got to be something I can use, something she's missed.

And then, I remember. Crawling onto my bed, I take hold of the corner of the curtain hanging above my bed. Hidden in the hem is a small piece of glass I'd found on the side of the road a few days ago. I knew it'd come in handy, so I stowed it where I knew she wouldn't look.

Within seconds, it's in my hand and carving a thick line down my forearm before I even realise what I'm doing.

The door swings open and Mum rushes in, a look of pure panic on her face. "Tracey, no! What have you done?" She runs to my side, grabbing my arm, and the glass slips from my grip. She brushes it to the floor and inspects my arm. "We need to stop the bleeding. I need my first aid kit."

I stare at her, knowing she's right, but hating that she's offering me no comfort. All the anger bubbles to the surface and I scream, "Can't you just be a normal mum for once! Stop trying to fix everything!"

She drops my arm, tears welling in her eyes as she brings her hand up to cover her mouth. "I'm sorry," she whispers through her fingers. After a beat, she reaches out for me, her eyes searching mine for approval. I nod, and she wraps me in her arms. "Shhh, it's going to be okay," she murmurs through her tears, and I realise I'm crying along with her. She pulls back and her eyes flick to my arm and back again. I can tell she's not comfortable just sitting here while I bleed, and for some reason that comforts me a little. Until a dull throb starts to register in my brain.

Why does it hurt this time? It's not meant to hurt. It's meant to take the pain away not make it worse.

My eyes lower to my arm now coated in blood. Droplets fall to the bedsheet beneath me, forming a small puddle. I look up at Mum in panic.

This wasn't meant to happen.

Biting her lip, she hesitates before ripping her sleeve from her shirt like some sort of superhuman being. "I'm sorry, I have to," she says as she tries desperately to wrap my wound, but the blood just seeps through, scenting the air with copper.

It's much deeper than I've ever cut before, and for the first time, I'm scared.

There's so much blood.

"Am I going to d-die?" I ask, looking to her for answers. I didn't mean to do it so deep. I wasn't thinking. She can fix this, right? She is Fix-It-Mum after all. She can fix anything.

"No, of course not." The warble in her voice makes me question whether she's telling the truth or not, but right now, I'll take her lies over the fear of death.

"I don't want to die, Mum." I shake my head, trying to make it all go away. The pain in my arm competes with the pain in my heart for attention, and I don't know what to do.

"I know, baby. Everything will be okay. I'm going to get you some help." She places my hand over the bandage already a deep crimson in colour and still dripping. "Hold this, I'll be right back."

With her hand covering her mouth, she runs out the door, and I hear her sob as she races through the house. I lean my head back against the wall, all my energy slowly draining from my body, making it impossible to keep my eyes open.

"...please hurry. There's so much blood..." The bed dips, and cool hands touch my face. "Baby, stay with me, okay? You need to stay with me. I love you. We're going to get through this."

I try to focus on her words, the words that sound so unlike my mother, but what I've longed to hear for so long.

I love you. We're going to get through this.

Janet

Chapter Eight

Hospital corridors are far from inviting. The stark white walls and squeaky linoleum floors don't scream out comfort as you'd expect to find in the one place you need it the most.

My daughter, my baby is through a set of swinging doors, out of my sight. I want to be with her, to hold her hand and tell her she's going to be okay, but they won't let me. She'd lost so much blood by the time the ambulance arrived, and she was whisked away from me before I could even say two words.

She needs me, and I'm not there.

I pace back and forth, rewrapping my cardigan tighter around me, trying to ignore the splatters of red dotting up my front; the reminder of the horror scene I'd walked in on. I don't know what I expected to find when I heard her cry out, but seeing her hacking at her arm with a lost look in her eyes was not it.

I don't want to die, Mum.

Her words haunt me, playing on repeat in my mind. My arms slink around my middle, clutching at my clothes in some sort of desperate attempt to hold myself together as I double over.

I can't lose her too.

"Janet?" His voice is like an echo of the past coming back to haunt me. A not-so-subtle reminder of what could have been. I suck in a deep breath, sobbing it out as I crumple to the floor in a heap, curling into a ball on my side. I can't deal with my ghosts when I need to be strong for Tracey.

"Janet?" Strong arms lift me, cradling me close. The familiar scent of Malcolm envelopes me as I'm rocked in a cocoon of warmth. I know it can't be him, he hasn't shown any interest in us since he left. I tell myself it's just my mind playing tricks on me, but I close my eyes and embrace the affection all the same. "I came as fast as I could."

I blink, turning my eyes up to see it *is* him holding me. I wasn't imagining it. "Malcolm?" My fist grips his sleeve, testing that he's really here and not just a figment of my imagination.

"She... Her arm... Oh God, there was so much blood." My head falls against his strong chest, and his arm circles around my waist, the other slipping behind my knees as he lifts me up.

"Shhh, I know, the hospital called me. It's going to be okay. We'll get through this." He carries me to the waiting room, sitting me on the couch beside him. I sniff and hiccup, trying to catch my breath while his hand rubs my back. It occurs to me this is the most intimate we've been in a long time, and I don't know how I feel about it. The comfort is nice, but it's also confusing.

"How did this happen?" His words hold no malice, but they sting all the same. How *did* this happen? It's a question I keep asking myself. How could I let this happen to our baby girl?

"I don't know what's going on with her lately. She's been so distant, withdrawn. I can't get through to her." I sob, once again wishing I'd done more to help her. Perhaps if I'd been more vigilant with her room searches, or forced her into counselling, we wouldn't be in this mess. I knew what she was doing, and I turned a blind eye, pretending she wasn't still cutting even though she kept a supply of sharp instruments in her room. What kind of parent does that?

"I'm sorry. I should've been there more. I thought I'd give you both some time to adjust. I didn't want to confuse things." He sighs, his fingers still tracing circles on my back. I know it means nothing, but something inside me wants to believe differently. Wants to grasp onto that tiny sliver of hope that maybe, just maybe, he means he didn't want to confuse things for himself. That perhaps being near us would make him realise what he's given up. That maybe he misses us.

What am I doing? I chide myself with a shake of my head. My daughter is in a critical condition and I'm dreaming of reconciling with the man who chose to walk away. No wonder she doesn't want anything to do with me.

I straighten myself up, pushing away from him and taking a seat opposite instead. I need the distance to clear my head.

"I'll talk to Maggie, see if she's got any insight."

Malcolm nods, leaning forward and resting his elbows on his knees. "Good idea. I can see if Kat has noticed anything too." His eyes flick up to mine, and he has the decency to appear ashamed. He takes a breath. "Janet, I really didn't mean—"

I hold my hand up to stop him. "Not here. Not now."

"Right, another time then?"

I don't even know what to say to him. Opening old wounds doesn't seem like such a good idea.

"Mr. and Mrs McLean?" A woman in pastel green scrubs stands in the doorway.

"We're not... um... doesn't matter." I wave a hand in the air, standing. "Is Tracey okay? Can we see her?"

"She's stable, but she lost a lot of blood. She has a cracked rib and broken nose. Rest is paramount for her right now." I nod, fresh tears springing to my eyes. "We'd like to keep her here for 48 hours for observation." She glances down at the pamphlets in her hand. "It's likely this has given her the scare she needs, but I'd recommend some counselling to help her work through whatever is going on." She holds them out to me, and I don't miss the way her eyes flick between us. "It might also be beneficial for you too. I know this can't be easy."

"Thank you." I stare at the pamphlet as the doctor's words sink in. "I'm sorry, did you say she has a cracked rib?"

What is going on with my Tracey?

"Yes, among other things. It looks as though she's been in a fight. Perhaps she's being bullied?"

"She hasn't said anything."

Have I been so wrapped up in myself that I didn't notice?

"I'm sure you're aware this isn't the first time she's cut. The scars on her abdomen and torso speak for themselves. I assume this is the first time it's gone this far?" My hand flies to my mouth as a sob breaks through. Malcolm moves to stand beside me, draping an arm around my shoulders. It feels forced, like it's all just an act for the sake of the doctor. Like he's trying to portray the image of a happy family, not offering any real support. With a tiny step to the side, I create a gap between our bodies. A small act of rebellion. Petty perhaps, but it's what I need to do to stay focused on what's important. Our daughter.

"She did once before, that I know of—"

"What? When?" Malcom takes a step back, staring at me. "Why didn't you tell me?"

I turn my eyes on him. "Take a guess." He blanches, stumbling backwards as if my words cause him physical pain.

"I had no idea."

I sigh. "I know. You weren't... around." I turn to the doctor. "I never saw cuts again, so I thought..." I let my words trail off, knowing them for what they are; a lie. I never saw cuts, that's true, but I certainly suspected she was still cutting. That's why I searched her room each day.

"People who self-harm often do so as a way to take back control of their emotions. They often express being overwhelmed. If she's being bullied, this could be why. Is there anything else going on at home? At school?"

I look to Malcom with tears in my eyes. "We're going through a separation. Could that be it?"

"It's possible. Has she voiced how she feels about it?"

"Not really, no. She just hides in her room and barely speaks to me." I shake my head, scrunching my eyes closed. "I was trying to give her space. But she was..." A sob breaks through, crushing my chest. "I should've known. I should've done more."

She reaches out to touch my arm. "It's not your fault. Self-harmers will do what they can to hide it. You can't blame yourself. She needs you to be strong right now."

Chapter Nine

I stare out the window, watching a group of birds fly back and forth from one tree to another. No cares in the world, just flitting about, letting their wings take them wherever they want to go. Sometimes I wish I could be a bird. Soaring through the sky with the wind in your face; it's got to be the most serene way to live. No separations, no teasing, no beat-downs. Just the open air, and the ability to crap on anyone who pisses you off. Sounds like bliss.

But no. I wasn't so fortunate. I'm stuck here in this hospital bed, wishing I was anywhere but here, even though I know it's the best place for me. They tell me I have a cracked rib, but they can't do anything about it. The pain is bearable mostly, so long as I don't move or breathe. My nose has been reset, and I have to wear a cast for the next few days. I haven't seen my face yet, but I'm sure I look like I've been in a warzone. Good thing the yearbook photos have already been taken.

I bet word has already got around school. Somehow the rumour mill always manages to find out. More ammunition for Kat and her cronies. She's probably out celebrating. After all, she's the one who told me to do it. I may not have meant to, but she won't care about that insignificance. All she cares about is making my life a living hell.

Pain draws my attention, and I suck in a sharp breath. My fingers have made short work on the stitches beneath the bandage on my arm. I didn't even realise I was doing it. Fresh blood gathers under my nails, and I try to wipe it off on my hospital gown.

There's a light tap on the door, and I quickly shove my hand under the blanket so they don't see the blood. Pain shoots up my side, and I wince.

"Do you feel up to some visitors?"

I plaster on a smile and nod. "Sure."

"Tracey?" Mum's voice is strained, and I can tell she's been crying. "How're you feeling?" She rushes to my side, taking my hand. Her eyes flit down to the bandage and a frown creases her brow. Without thinking, I pull my hand out from the blanket and yank on the bandage, pulling it back down to cover the stitches. She grabs my arm. "What did you do?"

I don't know what to tell her, what the correct answer is, so I settle with, "It was an accident." My eyes return to the window, unable to take the hurt reflecting back at me. Instead, I watch the birds, wishing I could fly away, while she sits there stroking my hand, pretending everything is okay.

"We should get someone to look at that," she says, pressing the buzzer beside my bed.

A nurse bustles in and cleans my wound then calls the doctor in to stitch me back up. She doesn't question me or berate me, just goes about her business, fixing me up again, while we sit in silence.

After they leave the room, Mum takes my hand again, clearing her throat. "Ah, your dad is here."

I return my gaze to her, my eyes wide in shock. "He is?"

She nods. "He's out in the hall. Should I send him in?"

"Okay." I can't help the smile that tugs at my lips just knowing he's actually here. For me.

Suck on that, Kat.

Mum tucks a hair behind my ear, cupping my face gently with her hand. "It's nice to see a smile on your face again." She leans forward, her lips brushing against my forehead before she stands. "I'll go tell him to come in, give you two some space." She pats my hand then turns away with a small sigh.

I still can't wrap my head around Mum being affectionate. It's surreal. Like all she was waiting for was for me to call her on it. All this time, I thought she didn't give a shit, but I guess she's been going through her own stuff. I was just too blinded by my own pain to notice.

"Mum?" I call out as she reaches the door.

"Mmm?"

"I'm sorry."

She frowns, and I swear her lip quivers. "No. I'm sorry. I haven't been the mum you needed or deserved. I wasn't... available to you, not fully." Her eyes glisten with unshed tears. "It's hard for me to be so open with my emotions, but it doesn't mean that I don't love you. I love you more than the air I breathe." She steps back towards the bed, and the dam breaks, tears streaking down her cheeks. "You're my whole world, Tracey, and I'm sorry you felt like you couldn't come to me." Her face crumples, and she looks as though she might fall to the floor. "I'm so, so sorry."

I can barely hold it together. We've never had the kind of relationship where we share our feelings with each other. It's almost too much to take, hearing her apologise to me and knowing what I've done.

A tear trails slowly down my cheek as I whisper, "It's not your fault, Mum. None of it." I sniff, swiping my hand across my face. "I acted like it was your fault, but I know it was mine. I'm the reason he left us."

"What? No! Why would you think that?" She settles back on the bed beside me, her hand grasping mine. "What happened between your father and I had nothing to do with you, sweetheart. Sometimes things just don't work between people."

"Then why doesn't he call or visit? Why do you avoid looking at me?"

"I-I don't..." She looks down at the sheet, folding and refolding the edge to make it smooth. "I don't know why he doesn't visit." She sighs, squeezing her eyes closed. "And I'm sorry I've been so distant. I don't blame you for anything, Tracey. It's all on me. I promise. I never meant to make you feel it was your fault."

"But you avoid me. I thought..."

She squeezes my hand. "There's something I need to tell you. Something I should've told you a long time ago."

"Okay?"

She takes a deep breath, letting it out slowly. "You had an older sister." The words slip off her tongue on a whisper.

"What?" *She can't be serious.* "For a minute there, I thought you said I had a sister."

She peeks up at me with a sad smile. "She would've been twenty if... Um..." She stops, dropping her head and taking a breath. "We were on holiday, your father and I with Serena, that was her name. You would've loved her." Her eyes take on a wistful look as she stares off to the side of me. "She looked a lot like you. She had the biggest brown eyes you've ever seen, and soft brown hair that fell in waves around her face. She was always smiling and talking." She chuckles at the memory. "I remember she used to try and sing Twinkle Twinkle Little Star, but it would come out Twinkle Sar, Wonder Sar."

I'm almost afraid to ask, but I have to know. "What happened to her?"

Her eyes dull and her bottom lip trembles. "We were at the river, walking over the rocky shore. She was so head-strong, stubborn, like you. She kept saying she could do it by herself, and pulling out of my grasp." A lone tear pools and trails down her cheek. "There was a large

72

boulder with a jagged edge on it. It was slippery, and she pulled away. She ran and slipped, cracking her head on the stone and slipping under the water. Your father dove in to save her, but the water was too swift. She'd floated downstream and he couldn't get a grip on her."

"Oh my god." I clutch my chest as tears prick my eyes.

"We found her, face down on the shingle about 200m down." She shakes her head as if trying to get the image from her mind. "She wasn't breathing." Closing her eyes, she takes a deep breath, huffing it out. "We tried to resuscitate her, but neither of us really knew how. Sh-she died." Mum points a finger at her chest. "It was my job to protect her, to keep her safe, and I failed. I couldn't help her."

The first aid kits.

Fix-It-Mum to the rescue.

It all makes sense now.

I reach out, placing my hand over hers. "It's not your fault, Mum. Kids do stupid things." I hold up my arm. "Case and point." It gets a small smile out of her.

"My head tells me that, but my heart," she holds her hand across her chest, "my heart tells me I should've protected her. I should've known how to save her." She raises her gaze to meet mine. "I should've saved you too."

"You *did* save me," I whisper.

Chapter Ten

"There she is." Dad's smile lights up the room as he slips through the door. "You gave us quite the scare, sunshine." The nickname from my childhood sends a wave of emotion through me.

"Hey, Dad." I nod at the chair beside the bed. "You can come closer."

His shoulders sag as if a weight has been lifted. "I wasn't sure if you'd want to see me." He takes a cautious step towards the chair, his hand running along the top. "I'm sorry I haven't been around much."

I shrug, unsure what to say to that. I'm glad he's here, and I want to forgive him, but something inside me isn't quite ready. Instead, I ask the question that's been plaguing me since Mum left the room. "Why didn't you tell me about Serena?"

Dad's eyes widen and he purses his lips. "She told you." It's more of a statement than a question. "I was wondering when she would."

"You could've."

He takes his time settling in the chair. "I know. Believe me, I thought about telling you a million times, but your mother made me promise."

"But why? She was my sister."

"When Serena died, a part of her died along with her. She was never quite the same." He leans forward, bracing his elbows on his knees. "The nurture gene is strong inside her, and when that happened, she blamed herself for not knowing how to save her. She built a wall around herself to protect her heart from hurting again."

"So she just forgot about her? Cast her aside? Where are the pictures? Where are her things?"

"It's not like that, Tracey. Your mother may seem like she's tough as old boots, but deep down she's fragile. She couldn't handle the constant reminder and made me take down all the pictures. Things were bleak for a while. And then you came along. Our little ray of sunshine." He smiles, taking my hand. "She got a little of that spark back in her eyes when you were born."

If I hadn't seen a different side to Mum today, I wouldn't have believed him. I wish I could've known her before she became bogged down with grief and guilt.

"Do you still have her pictures somewhere? Can I see them someday?"

"Of course. We packed them up, we didn't destroy them. I knew one day she'd be ready to face seeing them again. Perhaps she will be

77

now." He pulls his wallet from his back pocket. "I can show you a small picture I keep with me though." He rifles through, pulling out a worn square of paper. "Here."

I take it with shaking hands. The paper has creases all over it, as if it's been pulled out a thousand times before. In the centre is the smiling face of my sister. She looks just as Mum described; brown hair and big brown eyes, with a gappy grin. She's holding a bright yellow duck in her hands. I brush my fingers over the image, wishing I could've met her.

"She looks a lot like you did when you were her age." He retrieves another square of paper from his wallet. "See?"

My own face stares back at me, a matching toothy grin, brown eyes, and brown hair. The only difference is the toy in our hands. Instead of a duck, I'm holding my fluffy elephant. The one that sits on my pillow while I sleep.

"Your mum isn't always good at showing her emotions. She doesn't mean to hold you at arm's length. She really does love you, you know that, right?"

"I know."

"I know I didn't help things by walking away, and I'm sorry. I should've been there for you."

I hand back the pictures, swallowing back the lump in my throat. "Why *did* you leave? Was it something I did?"

He scoots forward in his chair, grabbing my hand. "No, of course not!"

"That's what she said too, but I don't understand why you didn't come back to see me if it wasn't my fault."

His head drops into his chest and his shoulders heave. "I never meant for any of this to happen." He tips his head, meeting my gaze. "But I promise you, it was nothing you did. It was all me."

I purse my lips, unsure whether I should say what's on my mind.

"What is it?"

"It's just," my eyes flick down to my bandaged arm and back up to his eyes, "Kat said you chose her over me."

"She what?" Dad sits up, a frown creasing his brow.

"She told me you didn't want me anymore, that you wanted a new family." My voice warbles and the sting of tears pricks my eyes. I turn my head away, back to the safety of the birds in the darkening sky outside.

"She... she said that? Oh, sunshine, why would you believe that?" He grasps my chin with his thumb and finger, pulling me round to face him. "I would never choose someone else over you."

"Then why didn't you come back?" Tears flow freely down my face now. I swipe them away, angry that I can't hold it in. Nothing he can say will make it better. He was the glue that held us together, and without him, I was lost. A lone raft floating on the rocky waves without an oar.

One little slice is all it will take.

A voice speaks quietly in the back of my mind, enticing me, coaxing me.

Just one little nick to take the pain away. No more emotions, no more feeling, just relief.

I don't care what he has to say anymore. All I can think about is getting him out of here so I can make it stop. The voices, the pain; I can't take it anymore.

"Sunshine. I—"

"Don't worry about it," I interrupt, forcing my lips into a half-smile as I wipe the last few tears from my face. "You're here now, right? That's what matters."

The relief on his face almost makes me feel guilty for my deception. Almost. I settle back into my pillow, letting my eyes drift closed. "I'm feeling kind of tired, Dad. Do you mind if I rest now?"

"Oh, of course." He pushes up from his chair. "I'll stop by later and check on you." His lips brush my forehead, and I smile again, knowing it's only a matter of minutes before I feel relief.

I wait until I hear the door close, then slowly peel my eyes open, making sure I'm alone. Once I'm sure, I sit up, scanning the room. There has to be something I can use. Something a nurse has left or...

A broken metal edging on the side of the bed catches my eye. I reach out, running my finger over the jagged end to check. It'll do.

Chapter Eleven

The door to Tracey's room swings open and Malcolm strides out. He crouches at my feet, his hand landing on my knee. "How are you doing? Tracey was asking about Serena. I know that must've been hard for you."

"I'm failing her as a mother." I hold my head in my hands. "You should've seen her face when I told her."

"You're not failing her. No one is perfect, and you did what you needed to do to get through it yourself." He waits a beat before speaking again. "I'm proud of you."

"Pfft," I scoff. "I'm not. She had a right to know, and I kept it from her. And you stuck by me even though you wanted to tell her." I lift my gaze to meet his. "I'm sorry I made you do that."

He places his hands over mine. "Stop. I'm a grown man. I could've fought to tell her, but I didn't. This isn't all on you." I search his eyes for any sign of trickery, but he seems genuine. "Look, let's not play the blame game, okay? Because right now, I can guarantee I'm rivalling you for the top spot." He nods his head toward her room. "What she needs is our support, not our guilt over what we should've done. We need to work together to get her the help she needs."

I nod. He's right. There's no point in going over the should-haves when our little girl is lying in a hospital bed. That helps nobody. "Okay." I pull out the pamphlet from the doctor. "I guess I'll call them."

He takes it from my hand. "I can do it." I purse my lips, and he holds a hand up to stop me from speaking. "Please. I know you like to take charge of everything, but let me help you. You don't have to do this alone. We're stronger together."

I don't know why it surprises me that he's willing to fight for her, but it does. It's funny how fourteen years of being a good father can be washed away by two months of not. But now isn't the time to dwell on our past. Tracey needs us, and I'd be stupid to push him away now.

"Thank you."

"You don't need to thank me. She's my daughter too." He stands, pulling his phone from his pocket.

"I should call Maggie too and let her know what's happened. I'm sure Tracey will want to see her."

His face drops and a frown creases his brow.

"What is it?"

"She said something in there, about Kat." His cheeks flush, and he glances down the corridor as if he can't face me. "I think she may be the one bullying her." His eyes fall to his feet then up to meet mine in a silent apology.

My heart thunders in my chest, but in light of our truce, I try to keep my voice even and without accusation. "Why would she do that?"

"I don't know, but I'm going to find out." With his phone to his ear, he wanders down the corridor for some privacy.

I pull my own out, searching for Maggie's number. It rings twice before a groggy-sounding voice answers, and I realise the lateness of the hour.

"Maggie, I'm sorry to wake you. It's Janet McLean."

"No worries, Mrs McLean. Is everything okay?"

"Um, not really, no." This is harder than I thought it'd be. I take a shaky breath. "Tracey's in the hospital."

There's a gasp followed by the rustling of sheets, and I can picture her sitting up in bed, her hair tousled with the innocence of the young.

"Oh my god. What happened? Was it Kat?"

I stare down the corridor, where Malcolm is pacing the floor. "I hope not." A sigh slips through my lips. "Truth is, I don't know what's going on with her right now. She came home with a broken nose and cracked rib, and I found her—" My voice catches in my throat as I begin to sob all over again. "She cut herself."

"She... what? I don't understand."

"She cut herself. On purpose. It's not the first time either."

There's a sniffle down the line. "I knew things were bad, and I tried to get her to tell you or talk to the teachers, but I didn't know she was doing that, I swear."

"I know. I'm not blaming you, Maggie. I just want to know what's going on with her. Why did you ask if Kat had done something? Is there something I should know?" I hold my breath, squeezing my eyes closed as if that will somehow make it easier to take.

Maggie sniffs, then lets out a long breath. "She's going to hate me for telling you this, but I don't care. Kat Goodall and her gang have been bullying her. She didn't want to say anything to upset you, and she thought if she ignored Kat and her friends, they'd leave her alone."

"But they didn't."

"No."

I turn my eyes to the ceiling, trying to find the strength to continue. "What exactly have they been doing?"

"Calling her names, following her, teasing her. They put gum in her hair the other day, that's why I cut it for her. She had a bruise on her shoulder after class the other day, but she tried to hide it from me because I keep telling her to talk to someone about it."

"How long has this been going on?"

"Umm, I think around two months, maybe more. It wasn't a big deal at the start, but Kat's gotten worse lately."

"Jesus." My hand flies to my mouth. *How could I be so blind to this? How could I not see it?*

"Is she going to be okay?" Her voice breaks, and I can tell she's trying to hold in her tears.

"Yes, but it's going to take some time. She's going to need our support."

"Okay. Can I... can I see her?"

"She's resting right now, but I'm sure she'd love to see you in the morning."

She huffs out a breath of relief. "Okay. Thanks, Mrs McLean."

Chapter Twelve

I barely slept last night. Not that it's any different to most nights lately. It is impossible to shut my brain down, like I've got to go over every single detail of my torment a thousand times. Sometimes I think I can see her standing outside my window, glaring at me. I spend most nights watching and waiting for her next move.

Now, the sun is peeking through the clouds, signalling a brand-new day. The birds are singing, trees rustling in the wind, and out the door, the corridor is coming to life. Nurses stride up and down the halls, buzzers ring, trolleys with squeaky wheels are trundled past.

Mum and Dad are both sound asleep on the recliners in opposite corners of the room. I guess they wanted to make sure I didn't hurt myself again.

My fingers graze the small ridge along my thigh where I'd cut last night. The relief had been instant, but it hadn't lasted more than a few seconds before guilt settled in the pit of my stomach.

Even in their sleep, my parents' faces are marred with worry. Knowing it's because of me makes that guilt swell until I feel like I'm going to be sick. I swing my legs over the edge of the bed, grabbing the IV drip to steady myself. With a quick glance over at my parents, I slip into the bathroom as quietly as I can. Just seeing the porcelain bowl has my stomach heaving, and I drop to my knees, gripping the edges as I throw up what little food I have in me.

I sit back, resting on my haunches as I stare at the ceiling with unseeing eyes. My breath comes in ragged gasps, the acidic smell of bile making me recoil. With shaking hands, I grasp the vanity beside me and pull myself up to stand.

The image that greets me in the mirror is not a pretty sight. Both eyes have black and blue bruising around them, the stark white bandaging on my nose making them seem darker. My chin is red and raw, and there is a split in my lip with dried blood caked on it. I lift my fingers to tentatively brush over my skin as I twist my face side-to-side. There's still blood under my nails from when I picked at my stitches.

Mum's voice in the back of my head tells me I should wash the cut from last night.

We don't want an infection now, do we?

Without thinking, I pull the string on my robe, letting it drop to the floor. A gasp flies from my mouth as I take in the road map of cuts across my body. I haven't dared to look before, and it's a shock to see them all at once. They travel up under my bra and along my ribs. Some run along the edge of my knickers on my hip bone. I look like a patchwork doll made up of criss-cross marks tarnishing my skin. I look broken, and that's exactly how I feel.

"Tracey? Is everything okay in there?" The door slides open a fraction. I don't bother to cover myself, too shocked to even move. Tears slide down my face as I meet her eyes in the mirror.

"Mum." My voice breaks, and I slam a hand over my mouth to stop the sob from coming out. I see her looking at me with agony written all over her face, but she doesn't say anything, just slips into the room and closes the door behind her. With tears in her eyes, she wraps her arms around me. I let her hold me, allowing my body to relax into her.

When she pulls back, she wipes the tears from my cheeks and brushes my hair behind my ears with a smile. She turns me back to the mirror. "What do you see?"

"Something ugly," I whisper.

She shakes her head. "You want to know what I see?" She gives my upper arm a squeeze. "I see someone who's fought a long time to be strong."

"I don't feel strong."

"That's only because you've been fighting for so long. But you don't have to fight on your own anymore." She bends to pick up my robe, handing it to me. "Your father and I are here for you. We'll get through this together, as a family."

I nod, taking hold of the flimsy fabric. Before I can put it on, there's something I need to do. I lift my eyes to hers, my lip trembling as I try to find the words. "I did it again. Last night." I show her the puckered line running up my thigh.

She doesn't tell me off or try to fix it. She simply nods and says, "Thank you for telling me." Her acceptance instantly sets me at ease, the guilt shedding like a second skin I've outgrown. I turn back to the mirror and try to see myself as she sees me. Not somebody flawed and useless, but somebody strong who just needs a little help.

"They say the first step is admitting you have a problem, right?" My fingers stray to the bandage wrapped around my arm. "I don't want to do it anymore. I want to get better." I meet her eyes in the mirror again, the eyes reflecting pride and adoration. "I want to feel again."

Chapter Thirteen

"Good morning, sunshine." Dad's grin beams at me from across the room. "You're looking more," he glances at Mum then back at me, "chipper. You've got more colour in your cheeks."

I roll my eyes. "They're bruises, Dad, but thanks. I do feel better today." Mum's hand runs down my arm, offering silent support as I walk back to the bed.

"Are you hungry? Shall I see if we can get you something to eat?" He stands, stretching his arms above his head with a sigh.

"Thanks, that'd be nice." I flop down on the bed, staring at the tiny flowers covering my gown. "Do you think I need to keep wearing this?" I lift the fabric, letting it fall back into my lap. "I mean, I'm not really bedridden."

"I don't see why you couldn't get changed. Your clothes from yesterday are... um... How about I get Maggie to bring you something to wear? She was going to pop in anyway."

My eyes widen and I freeze in place. "She is?" I dip my chin, pulling my split lip between my teeth with a hiss. "Did you tell her? What I did?"

The mattress dips as Mum perches beside me. She places her hand over mine, nudging me with her shoulder. "I did. She's your best friend, Tracey. She wants to help you just as much as we do."

"I know. It's just embarrassing, you know?" Tears prick my eyes, and I swallow the lump forming in my throat.

"I'm sure she doesn't see it that way. She cares about you, and she just wants you to feel better. We all do."

Staring down at my bandaged arm and the cuts hidden beneath, I know she's right. Maggie's been trying to help me for weeks, but I refused. "I want to feel better too," I whisper. "I just don't know how." I tap a finger against my forehead. "I don't know how to stop the thoughts or the voices, and the urge is so strong sometimes, Mum." I glance at her through my tears. "It's so loud I can't think straight."

With a trembling chin, Mum reaches her hand up to cup my jaw. "That's where your support network comes in." She smiles though I know she's struggling. "You have me and your father, and Maggie of course. But there are other people who want to help too. Trained professionals who can help you navigate all these emotions and urges. In fact, I spoke to someone last night while you slept. She's going to pop in later for a chat."

"A shrink."

"A counsellor. She comes highly recommended."

Fix-it-Mum to the rescue again. Only this time, it feels good to know she's got my back.

"Will you stay with me when she's here?" I peer up at her, and she seems to dissolve, her body slumping forward as she threads her fingers through mine.

"Of course I will." She brings my hand up to her mouth, her lips brushing against my palm. "Anything you want."

"Thanks." I lean my head on her shoulder.

"Knock knock." Dad pokes his head in through the door. "I, ah, found someone in the hallway who'd like to speak to you." He chuckles uncomfortably, and his eyes dart to Mum then back to me.

His awkwardness makes me suspicious, and I narrow my eyes. He offers a shrug, and it suddenly becomes clear.

How could he do this to me?

My stomach drops as I shake my head, silently pleading with him, but he steps aside, holding the door open.

All the air seems to leave the room as she steps through the door. Kat Goodall.

I clutch at the loose collar of the hospital gown as if it's now choking me. She stands there, gaping at me with an odd expression. Not the usual hate I see directed my way, but... could it be guilt?

Dad puts his hands on her shoulders and urges her forward. "Kat has something to say to you. Don't you, Kat?"

She nods, her eyes glued to the bandage on my arm.

"Janet, let's give them a minute, shall we?"

Mum seems reluctant to leave, but she does, giving me an encouraging smile before she walks through the door, closing it behind her.

Kat cautiously steps closer, her hands finding the back of the chair to my right. "Hi."

Her voice is soft, gentle, so unlike what I've become accustomed to.

"Hey." I fiddle with the hem of my gown.

"Does it hurt?" Her eyes flick over my bruised face and bandaged arm before settling on the space above my head. She can't even bear to look at me, so I don't bother answering her question.

"I didn't mean it, you know? When I said... what I said..." Her mouth twists to the side as her head tilts up to the ceiling. "Shit." She takes a few deep breaths before looking at me. *Are those tears I see?*

"I didn't really think you'd do it." Her voice catches in her throat as she waves her arm towards mine.

"I didn't do it for you." My fingers tremble as I lift one side of my gown, exposing my bruised ribs with the criss-cross patterns. Her eyes widen, and she takes a step forward.

"Why? Why would you do that to yourself?" Her hand reaches out as if she wants to touch them, but I pull back, covering myself up again.

"Because it's easier to focus on physical pain than it is to feel what I really feel." She looks at me like I'm crazy. I shrug. "You wouldn't get it. And you shouldn't. No one should feel like this."

She takes a seat, pursing her lips. "So, it wasn't anything I did?"

"Believe me, what you did was rat-shit, and it certainly didn't help. You made my life miserable." I level her with a stare. "But you didn't make me do this. I made me do this. As much as you'd like to think it, you don't hold that much power over me." I don't even realise I feel that way until the words are out of my mouth.

She's not to blame. She was an excuse.

I swivel and lean my back against the pillow, swinging my legs up onto the bed. "In case you hadn't noticed, I've kind of been going through some shit at home. You were just the last nail in the coffin."

Kat nods, staring at her lap. "Yeah, I know. And I know I couldn't have helped the situation."

She almost sounds regretful, and it takes everything in me not to scoff at her words.

"Ever since your dad moved in, I just felt this overwhelming hatred toward you, you know? Like every time I saw you, this anger would bubble up until I couldn't take it anymore. It just kind of spewed out of me." She glances up at me, her lips twisted to the side. "I was so horrible to you, and you don't even seem mad."

"Oh, I have been. But this—" I hold my arm out between us, "—this scared the shit out of me. I've been cutting for a while, but I've never gone that deep before." My chest tightens as I think of what I put Mum through last night. What I put myself through. "I don't want to be that person anymore. I shouldn't have to bleed so I can deal with things, no matter how shitty they are." I glance at her with a small smile. "I have to take responsibility for my own actions to move forward."

She throws her arms into the air. "See? You're just so... perfect." Her brow creases as she leans forward. "You should hate me. You shouldn't even want me in the same room as you. That was me, right?" She points at my face. "I broke your nose."

"And cracked my rib."

"And cracked your rib. But still, you sit here talking to me about moving forward, like you forgive me or something. What's your deal?" She folds her arms across her chest, her knee bobbing up and down, and for the first time, I can see she's hurting too.

"Why is that so hard to believe? That I'd forgive you. Why are you so angry?"

"Because! Because even after everything I've put you through, you're still the perfect child he raves about." She waves her arm towards the door. "All he ever talks about is you and how wonderful you are. How intelligent you are, and how proud he is. He loves you more than anything... and... and my dad couldn't even stick around long enough to see my first birthday."

I can't quite fathom what she's saying. "This was all over my father loving me?" I raise my brow. "You were jealous?"

"I just wanted him to notice me, you know? I wanted *someone* to see me." Her bottom lip quivers, and she turns her head to the window, avoiding my gaze.

We have more in common than I thought.

"I see you, Kat. And I guarantee, he does too. You just have to let him in."

A sharp laugh bursts from her mouth followed by a snort. "There you go again, being all perfect." This time she grins at me, and I can't help but grin back.

"What can I say? You can't fight perfection."

Chapter Fourteen

"Tracey McLean?" A curvy woman with a bright smile and kind eyes stands beside the reception desk holding a clipboard. I raise my hand and stand. Mum does too. "This way please." The woman leads us down the hall to a small room painted in white, with one wall made up entirely of bookshelves, crammed full of books. Beside her desk is a window with blinds, a light breeze making them sway.

She gestures towards the seats and closes the door. "I'm Cassidy Rae, a mental health nurse. I spoke on the phone with Mr. McLean a few days ago?" She looks at her notes then back at me.

I glance at Mum, who nods. "Yes, that's right."

"Okay. I understand we had a bit of a scare?" Again, she looks at me.

"Um, yeah." I hold my arm up. It's no longer bandaged but small strips of plaster hold my healing wound together. I chew at the inside of my cheek.

Cassidy leans forward, resting her elbows on her knees. "You're doing a brave thing by being here. It's not easy to admit you need help, and I want you to know what a huge step this is. You should be proud of yourself."

I nod, but it doesn't feel like something to be proud of.

"Can you tell me a bit about what happened? What's been going on for you lately?"

I hesitate, and she offers a smile. "Everything you say in this room, stays in this room. This is a safe place, okay?"

Mum takes my hand, encouraging me. I gulp in a deep breath and explain everything from Dad leaving to Kat's torments, and Mum's distance. I tell her how I feel when I cut, and how I feel after. How I yearn for the relief it brings, and then hate myself for having no self-control. It all flows out, one after the other, like a tap that can't turn off. And when there's nothing more to say, I lean back in my seat, both exhausted and relieved.

Cassidy nods, adding a few scrawls to her notes. "That's quite a lot to be dealing with all at once. I can see why you would be feeling overwhelmed."

Having her acknowledge it gives me an odd sense of satisfaction. It has been a lot.

"Can you tell me what's going on inside your body when you start feeling that you need to harm yourself? Where do you feel it most?"

My hand instantly goes to my chest. "In here. It gets tight, like I can't breathe." I glance at Mum, who gives me a reassuring smile. "And in here." I tap the side of my head. "It gets loud."

Cassidy makes more notes.

"Tell me, Tracey, what do you like to do for fun? What activities do you really enjoy? Singing? Drawing? Going for walks?"

I shrug. "I like going for walks, I guess. And learning interesting facts."

"That's great." Cassidy smiles. "I know it's not always going to be possible, but when you start to feel that tightness in your chest, do you think you could take yourself for a walk around the block to recentre yourself? Or flip through a textbook for some fun facts? It doesn't need to be big, just something to distract yourself enough that you move past the urge."

I shuffle in my seat. "Yeah, I guess I could try that."

"Something else that can help, is writing down how you feel. Whether it's in a journal, or a letter, it can be very therapeutic. Sometimes we need to voice those emotions for them to have less power. Does that make sense?"

It *did* feel better after I told her everything. "Yeah, it does."

"And if you find you're not in a situation where you can take off for a walk or do one of these activities – say, in class, then perhaps some breathing exercises might help too." She adjusts herself in her seat. "Try it with me. Take a deep breath in through your nose for the count of five, then slowly out through your mouth."

I follow along, counting in my head.

"Good. That might be one for you to try too, Mrs McLean." Cassidy smiles at Mum. "Sometimes, as parents, we go straight into fix-it mode or even into anger because we don't understand, and using our breath can help you focus on what Tracey needs."

"Okay. I can do that." Mum nods. "I know I haven't been doing this the right way, and you're right in saying I don't understand it all. That's what frustrates me, because I just want to make it all better."

Cassidy reaches out and places a hand on Mum's arm. "You're not doing anything wrong. Being a parent is hard under any circumstances, and when you don't understand what your child is going through, it can be confronting. By bringing her here and showing her you support her, you're doing exactly what you should be."

Mum nods as she rummages through her bag for a tissue. Cassidy hands her a box. "You might find you benefit from some sessions of your own too."

Mum glances at me. "I think that would be a good idea, actually."

"We can discuss that after we're done in here if you like." Cassidy smiles then turns back to me. "I have one more activity I find helps. It's one that focuses on the senses. So you look around you and find five things you can see, four things you can hear, three things you can touch, two things you can smell, and one thing you can taste. You can do this activity anywhere, and it helps redirect your brain away from the intense emotion you're feeling." She finds a slip of paper and hands it to me with a pen. "Now, I want you to write down two things we've discussed that you're going to try when you're at home."

I write down the senses and the breathing exercise then hand it back to her. She waves it away.

"That's for you to take with you. To remind you." She places her notes on her desk and crosses her legs. "You've done really well today, Tracey. We've gone through a lot, and I know it can be hard to take it all in, that's why you're going to just try two of the suggestions this week, okay?"

I nod, shoving the piece of paper in my pocket.

"I'd like to see you weekly, sometimes with Mum and sometimes by yourself so we can work through some exercises." She stands, walking towards the door and opening it. "It was so lovely to meet you both."

Janet

Chapter Fifteen

The attic ladder thunks onto the floor in front of me. It's been quite some time since I've been up there, probably before Tracey was born, if I'm honest.

The ladder creaks as I press my foot tentatively on each rung before placing my full weight on. A thick layer of dust has accumulated over the boxes and floor. It floats on the air as I move around the room, searching for the box in question.

Tucked away at the back, behind the wooden bassinet and rocking horse, are two boxes labelled Serena. I drag them under the light in the centre of the room, dusting my hands on the back of my pants.

Circling the boxes, I let my fingers trail across the lid, leaving a line in the dust. If I'm to help Tracey through this, I need to face up to my own demons and accept what happened was out of my control. On some level, I know this, but there's another level that wants to condemn me for all eternity for not being able to protect my baby. My Serena.

I flick the lid open to reveal the pink knitted blanket my own mother had made when she found out we were expecting. Serena had been wrapped in it from the moment we left the hospital to the day we said our last goodbyes. When I lift it from the box, I bring it to my nose, inhaling. Her scent no longer clings to the fabric though. It's been tucked away up here for too long.

A tear slides down my cheek. It was silly to think it would still smell of her after all these years but think it, I did. Now that smell is lost to me.

Placing the blanket beside me, I peer back in the box to find her baby album. In the pocket of the front cover is the hospital bracelet from her birth and a tuft of hair from her first haircut. I flick through the pages, my fingers stroking each image of her chubby cherub face. A sob forces its way from my chest and throat, and I tilt my head skyward, keening softly.

"Mum?"

The ladder creaks, and I quickly wipe my eyes and close the album. Tracey's head pops through the hole, twisting from side-to-side.

"What are you doing up here?" she asks, pulling herself fully in.

I lift the flap of the top box so she can see her sister's name printed neatly in permanent marker.

"Oh." She hesitates, then moves towards me, dropping into a cross-legged position. "Can I see?" She points at the album still cradled in my arms, and I hand it over with a nod.

The spine crackles as she bends it back. I cuddle the blanket into my chest as if it can protect my heart from breaking all over again.

Tracey runs her finger across each page, her eyes taking in every last detail. The hint of a smile forms on her lips as she comes to a close-up of Serena's gummy grin. She was always such a happy, smiley baby.

While she pores over the album, I turn back to the box. A teething ring, fluffy pink bear, and a mobile of stars and planets sit on top of several framed photos. I push the toys aside and grab the first of the photos. The frame is silver and engraved with Serena McLean, 24.11.80. It had been a gift from Malcolm's parents. We have a similar one on the mantle with Tracey's name and birth date, and a photo of her only two days old, snuggled in a onesie with a hood and bear ears.

The frame has dulled, but Serena's dark eyes still grab my attention easily, and I'm instantly transported to the days after her birth when this photo was taken. I was exhausted after being up all night with her feeding every hour, and Serena had finally settled in my arms, staring up at me as if for the first time. It was that moment I truly felt like a mother.

The next image is one taken in a mall studio where Serena is propped against soft toys inside a small wooden wheelbarrow. It had taken half an hour just to get her to stop crying enough for them to snap a few shots. Her eyes are red-rimmed, but she's grinning, her nose scrunched up and her two front teeth on display. It's my favourite photo of her.

Tracey closes the album and puts it on the floor in front of her. She threads her fingers together in her lap. "I wish I could've known her."

I nod, handing her the framed images. "I wish you could've known her too."

"Do you really think I look like her?" She studies the grinning girl before her.

"I do." Unfolding my legs, I rise to stand. "Come on, let's find somewhere to hang these."

Tracey twists her head up to face me. "Really?"

"Yeah." I hold my hand out for the frames. "I never should've hidden them away."

Chapter Sixteen

"How's it feel being back at school?" Maggie holds the door open for me as I walk through to our lockers. Dropping our bags to our feet, we unlock the small wooden boxes and shuffle around what's needed for first period.

"It's kind of weird, to be honest." I glance over my shoulder. "I keep waiting for the insults to come."

"Yeah, it has been awfully quiet. Kat even came and sat with me the other day. She was actually being nice for a change." Her eyes widen and her lip curls. "It's like we stepped into an episode of the *Twilight Zone* or something."

I can't help but laugh at the face she's pulling, but I understand what she's getting at. The past few months have been an absolute nightmare, and to have everything come to a grinding halt is surreal.

"I guess we'd better get used to it now that Kat and I have a truce."

Maggie shakes her head. "It's still weird." Zipping her bag up, she slings it onto her shoulder and slams her locker closed. "So, how's everything else, anyway?" She nods towards my arm.

"One week cut free." I smile, raising the sleeve of my jersey so she can see.

"Trace, that's awesome! I'm so proud of you." She flings her arms around my neck, squeezing tight. "I'm not gonna lie, you really scared me. When your mum rang, I thought I'd never see you again." She pulls back, scrunching her nose. "I'm glad you're better."

"I wouldn't go that far. It's only been a week. But it's a start. And counselling helps."

"Well that's good." She nods then stops me with a hand on my arm. "Um, I wanted to say sorry to you too."

I frown. "What for?"

"For telling your mum what was going on. I know I promised I wouldn't say anything, but when she said you were in hospital, I freaked out."

"Mags, it's okay. You don't have to apologise for that. I should never have put you in that position." I nudge her with my elbow. "I should've listened when you told me to tell someone."

She holds her hands up in a half-shrug. "Well... I mean, I have been known to have some pretty good ideas in the past."

I chuckle along with her. It feels good to laugh again. "It was a great idea, and I'm glad you did it."

"Really?"

"Really." I link my arm through hers as we stroll down the corridor towards our first class.

As we pass the girls' toilets, loud voices shout out, and it sounds as though someone is crying. I look at Maggie with raised brows, and we stop outside the door, listening.

"Don't tell me to calm down!"

My eyes widen. "Is that Kat?" I whisper, and Maggie nods.

"I think so."

Before I can think too hard, I push the door open and find Kat backed up against the wall with a knife against her wrist and red-rimmed eyes. Across from her, in front of the stalls are her friends. One has her hands held out in front, as if warding Kat off, and the others cling to her sides.

"Kat?" I take a step forward, and her eyes find mine. "What's going on?"

Her eyes flicker to me then to the knife in her hand, and she seems to lose steam. Her hand shakes, and a tear trails down her cheek.

Any other day I'd think she was making fun of me, but the look in her eyes, and the tears tracking down her face say otherwise. I move towards her, holding my hand out.

"Give me the knife, Kat."

She shakes her head, her feet shuffling against the linoleum floor. "I can't," she whispers.

"You can." I edge closer. "You don't want to do this. Trust me."

Raising my arm, I slowly peel back my sleeve and show her the scarred welts that adorn my once flawless skin. "I'll have these for life. You don't want that." I take another step closer.

Her eyes dart to me then to the girls now behind me. "They said it's my fault." She nods at my arm. "That I went too far."

"We talked about this, remember? It's not your fault. I did this to myself." I glance back at the group of girls. "If you think Kat's to blame, then you can turn that pointing finger towards yourselves too, because you all treated me like crap." I make a point of meeting each of their eyes. "Every single one of you." I turn back to Kat. "But no one held a blade to my skin, but me. I did that all by myself. You wanna blame someone, blame me."

"But you wouldn't have done it if she hadn't started it," one of the girls pipes up.

Kat's face crumples in on itself, and she presses the sharp edge harder into her skin.

"That's not true, Kat." I reach towards her, my palm up. "Give me the knife."

She stares down at her arm and the knife pressed into her flesh as if she can find the answer there.

"I know it hurts to have your friends speak to you and about you like this, but this isn't the way. Believe me. It only makes things worse."

"I didn't mean for any of this. I just wanted him to notice me," she whispers.

"I know, Kat, and he does. And you know what? So do we. Right, Mags?" I wave my arm behind me, and Maggie comes to stand beside me.

"That's right. Who cares what these girls say? You can come hang out with us."

Kat jerks her head back, her brow creased. "I can?"

"Of course." I wiggle my fingers. "Just give me the knife first, okay?"

Her hands drop to her sides, the knife slipping from her fingers. There's a collective sigh of relief, and behind me, the girls shuffle their feet.

"You really don't blame her? Or us?" one of them asks, as if the world doesn't make any sense.

"I don't blame you for what I did to myself, no. But the way you treated me was pretty shit, you have to admit that."

She looks down at her feet, nodding her head. "Yeah, you're right. I'm sorry."

"It's okay, just, you know, think about it before you start tormenting someone else. You never know what people are going through." Turning back to Kat, I take her hand and pull her into a hug. "You're going to be okay, Kat."

Her arms tighten around me, and she buries her face in the crook of my neck. "Thank you."

Chapter Seventeen

When Tracey comes home from her first day back at school since the incident, I'm waiting in the kitchen for her with a coffee in my hand. I try to make it seem as if I haven't been waiting here for the past fifteen minutes, counting down the last second. Watching her walk out the door this morning was one of the hardest moments of my life. I've never wanted to wrap her in cotton wool so much as I did right then, but she proved how resilient she is, waving with a big grin on her face as she trudged down the drive.

"Hey, Mum," she says as she walks through the door. I search her face for any signs of animosity, but there are none. In fact, she seems more at ease than I've seen her in a long time.

"How was your day? Was it good to be back?" I force myself to take a sip of my drink and not run and pull her into my arms.

"It was... interesting," she says cryptically, then goes on to explain what happened with Kat in the bathrooms.

My heart jumps into my throat at the thought of Tracey having to talk a friend off a cliff like that, especially so soon after being in hospital herself. Part of me is cross at Kat for putting her through that, but I'm also coming to understand how hard it is to control all these emotions coursing through our bodies at any one time. I made the decision to force mine down and shut everyone out, but that wasn't a healthy decision. I can hardly blame Kat for thinking she had no other options left.

Instead, I take a breath and brush a strand of hair behind Tracey's ear. "I'm glad you were there for her. Are you okay?"

She purses her lips as if considering, then nods. "Yeah, I think I am." She clears her throat then steps towards me, slowly wrapping her arms around my waist and pressing her cheek to my shoulder. "I'm sorry for everything, Mum."

My hands come up to stroke her hair, and I kiss the top of her head. "It's okay, sweetheart. I'm sorry too."

When she pulls back, her eyes are glossy. "I guess I never really thought about what it was like for you before. But seeing Kat do that..."

I nod. "It made it more real?"

"Yeah. I was really scared for her."

"But the main thing is you stayed calm and you were there for her." With my thumb and forefinger, I raise her chin. "I'm really proud of you, Tracey. I know that wouldn't have been easy."

"It wasn't."

"And I know you want to help her, but the best thing we can do is talk to your dad and her mum, and get her the help she needs from someone else, okay?"

She frowns. "But I don't mind helping."

"I know you don't, and I love that about you, but you are my priority, and we need to focus on getting you better first. You can be there for her, but you can't shoulder this for her. You need to help yourself before you can help others."

She seems to think it through, her eyes landing on the framed photo of Serena she helped me hang in the weekend. She pulls her lips in between her teeth then nods. "We work on ourselves so we can be there for others."

I smile. "Exactly."

"So, are you going back to see Cassidy too then?" She quirks her brow, a smirk on her face.

"As a matter of fact, I am. I'm booked in to see her after you tomorrow."

She beams up at me, and for the first time in a long time, I see the little girl she once was. "That's great, Mum."

"Yeah." I smile, ruffling her hair like I used to. "It is."

Acknowledgements

This was originally part of the Scars to your Beautiful anthology that was released in 2018. I had always intended on extending it out to give the characters a little more growth, and I finally found time to do so.

It wasn't an easy piece to write back in 2018, and it was still quite difficult coming back to it now, all these years later. This story, though fiction, has personal meaning to me. Our family went through a rough time involving self-harm, and with the help of the Mental Health Foundation, we were able to band together and pull through.

Once again, self-harm became a part of our story this year, and I felt it was the right time to get this out there. So many people struggle with this and other mental health issues, and we need to have more conversations around it.

With that in mind, I'd like to take a moment and thank everyone who stood by us, offered support, and words of kindness at those times. It was very much appreciated, and I don't think I could've made it through without you.

Without naming anyone, thank you for finding the strength to work towards getting better. I love you and I'm so proud of you.

To everyone I've had the pleasure of meeting and bonding with over this story, I thank you too. It was a hard one to write, but it was also therapeutic to get out some of those emotions. Being able to reach others with my words, and bring these stories to light, means a great deal to me.

Thank you to Aria Peyton, who invited me to take part in the original anthology. Without her, I don't know if this story would have come about.

And, as always, thank you to my friend and proofreader, Trina. You've been with me from the very start, and you were with me through this time of my life too, and I honestly don't think I would've had the courage to write any of these stories if it weren't for you having my back. Love you, chick.

We are in a troubling time in the world today, and looking after our mental health is so important to do when everything else seems to be falling apart. I've struggled with depression and anxiety over the past few years myself, and I've been so lucky to have such a great support network around me. If you are finding it hard and need someone to talk to, please reach out to your local mental health foundation, helplines, or doctors. There's no shame in asking for help.

Love

Stacey xxx

About the Author

Stacey Broadbent is a multi-genre author from New Zealand. She writes under three different names and a variety of genres, so there is something to suit most tastes. You can find her LGBTQIA reads under the name Cyan Tayse, and children's books under the name Stacey Jayne.

An avid reader and lover of all things bookish, Stacey has made it her goal to share about her favourite authors and books she's read, while also building her own publishing story. She is a qualified proofreader and is embarking on a new journey of study - Library and Information Skills.

She is a member of the Unhinged Kiwi Booktalk discord group, and a great bunch of Canterbury based bookstagrammers. Her TBR is never-ending, and though she struggles to keep up with it, she continues to add more.

As well as reading, her hobbies include LEGO, cross-stitch, crochet, and diamond art, and you can often find her sharing about her latest project on TikTok.

If you feel like stalking her, here are the links!

www.staceybroadbent.com/

www.facebook.com/StaceyBroadbentAuthor

www.amazon.com/author/staceybroadbent

Goodreads: https://goo.gl/YJ6dXa

www.instagram.com/authorstaceybroadbent/

www.bookbub.com/authors/stacey-broadbent

www.tiktok.com/@authorstaceybroadbent

Broken

Other Books by Stacey Broadbent

<u>Standalone</u>

Never Judge a Book

Emma

Deep Heat

Lady Luck: A Deep Heat bonus novella

Fever

A Christmas Tail

Broken

Awesome Applesauce

<u>A Step in Time series</u>

Dancing through the Storm

Dancing in Circles

Dancing with Destiny

A Step in Time: the complete series

Super Mum series

Frazzled

Frazzled and Frumpy

Frazzled, Frumpy and Fabulous!

Super Mum: the complete series

Dark sins novellas

Sins of the Flesh

Mine

Hellhounds MC

Cut Loose

Break Loose

Let Loose (coming soon)

Short Stories and Poetry

Musings, Mournings, and Misadventures

Musings, Mayhem, and Mystery

Musings, Magic, and Mischief

Musings of a Writer: the complete collection

Anthologies

Scars to your Beautiful

Witching Hour: Vices and Virtues

The White Ribbon Collection

Key to my Heart

A Touch of Inspiration

No Place Like Home

Serendipity

Lucky Star

Hellhounds

www.ingramcontent.com/pod-product-compliance
Lightning Source LLC
Chambersburg PA
CBHW022026170626
46808CB00003B/1075